Calef Brown here. May I tell you something? I love to draw! It's my favorite thing to do, anytime, anywhere. I sketch and doodle with pens, pencils, markers, and brushes. I usually start with an outline, or a simple shape—a circle, a triangle, maybe a funky trapezoid. Then it's time for lots of lines—thin lines, thick lines, zigzags, loops. Eyes and noses. Ears and mouths, wings and paws. Whiskers. Fins. Wheels?

By the way, I can be a little forgetful, so you may see a few creatures that were not completed. Could you please do me a favor? Finish those drawings for me as soon as you see one. Otherwise they just look odd. Thank you! So jump right in! Follow some of my drawings, if you'd like, combine them, or feel free to make up your own fantastical creations!

Have fun!

Drawing snails is easy and fun.

Begin with a circle for the shell. Then a body, which is shaped like a letter J. Then a head and some antennae. Draw a face. Maybe a cat snail, a dog snail, a crocodile snail. A whatever-you-can-imagine snail!

Decorate the shell!

Spirals, stripes, zigzags, or circles! Diamonds, squares, loops, or ovals! All of the above!

Snails, snails, and more snails!

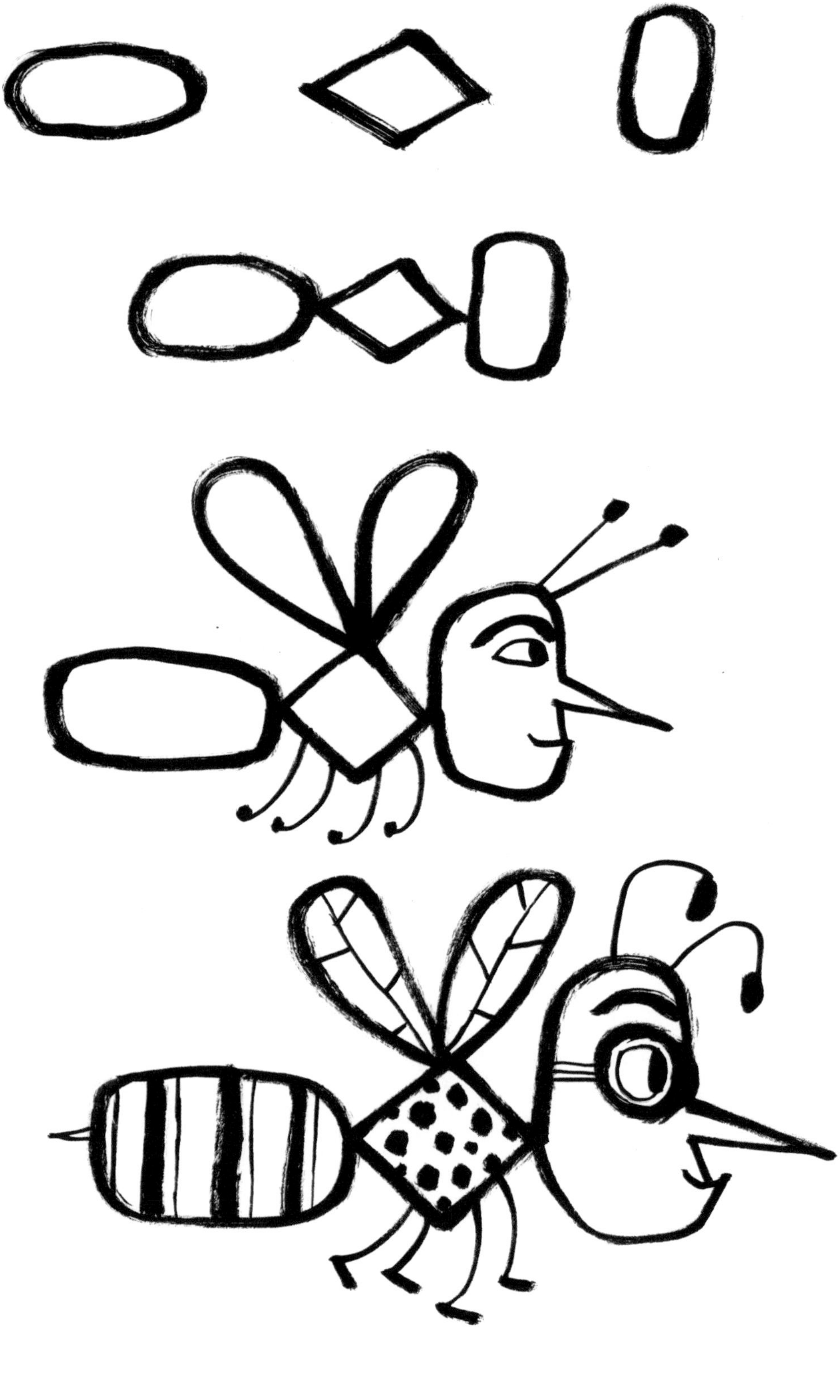

INSECT, assemble!

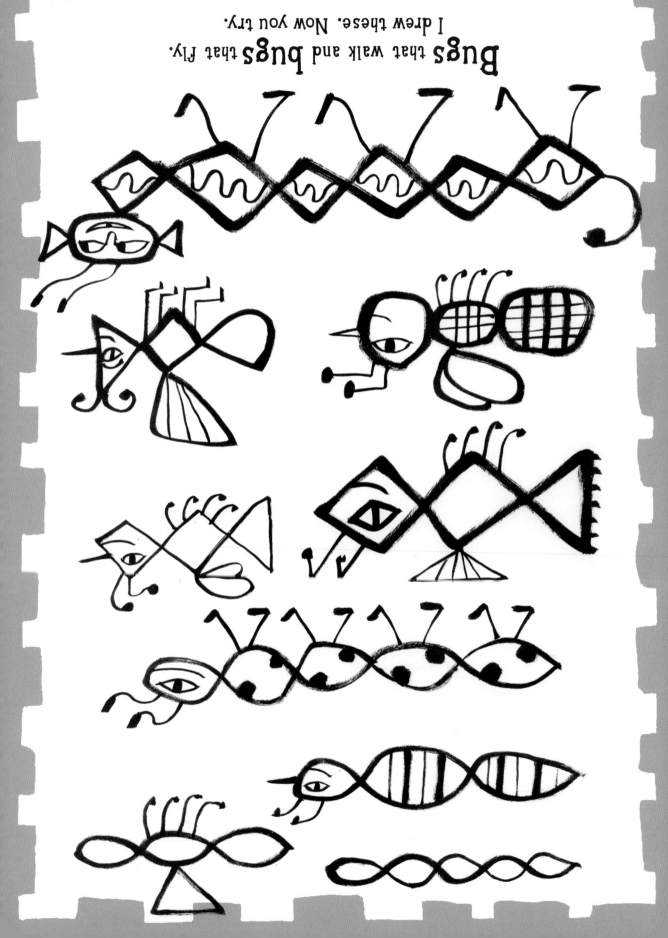

Draw a beetle.

One, two, three.

Start with one of these shapes here,
and create a crusty crab. Watch out, they
can be grouchy. And they pinch...OUCH!

Why not add to the Catassortment?

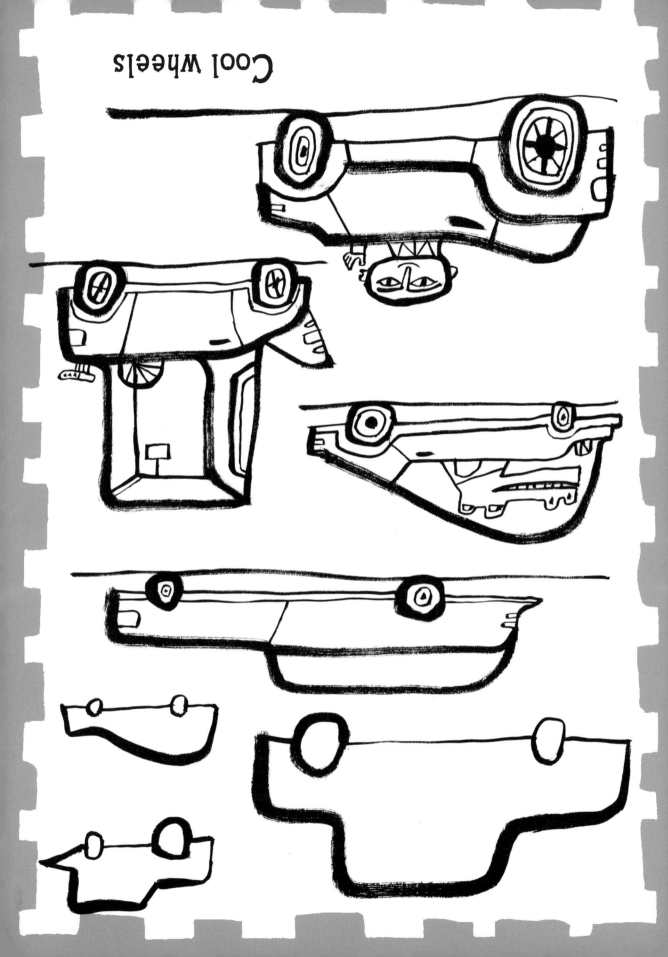

Li'l elephants.
Known to some as
Lillephants.

Snowbear, snowcat, snowpup, snowcroc.
(Clockwise, from top.)

Fluttering off to East Somewhere.

Who will they meet when they get there?

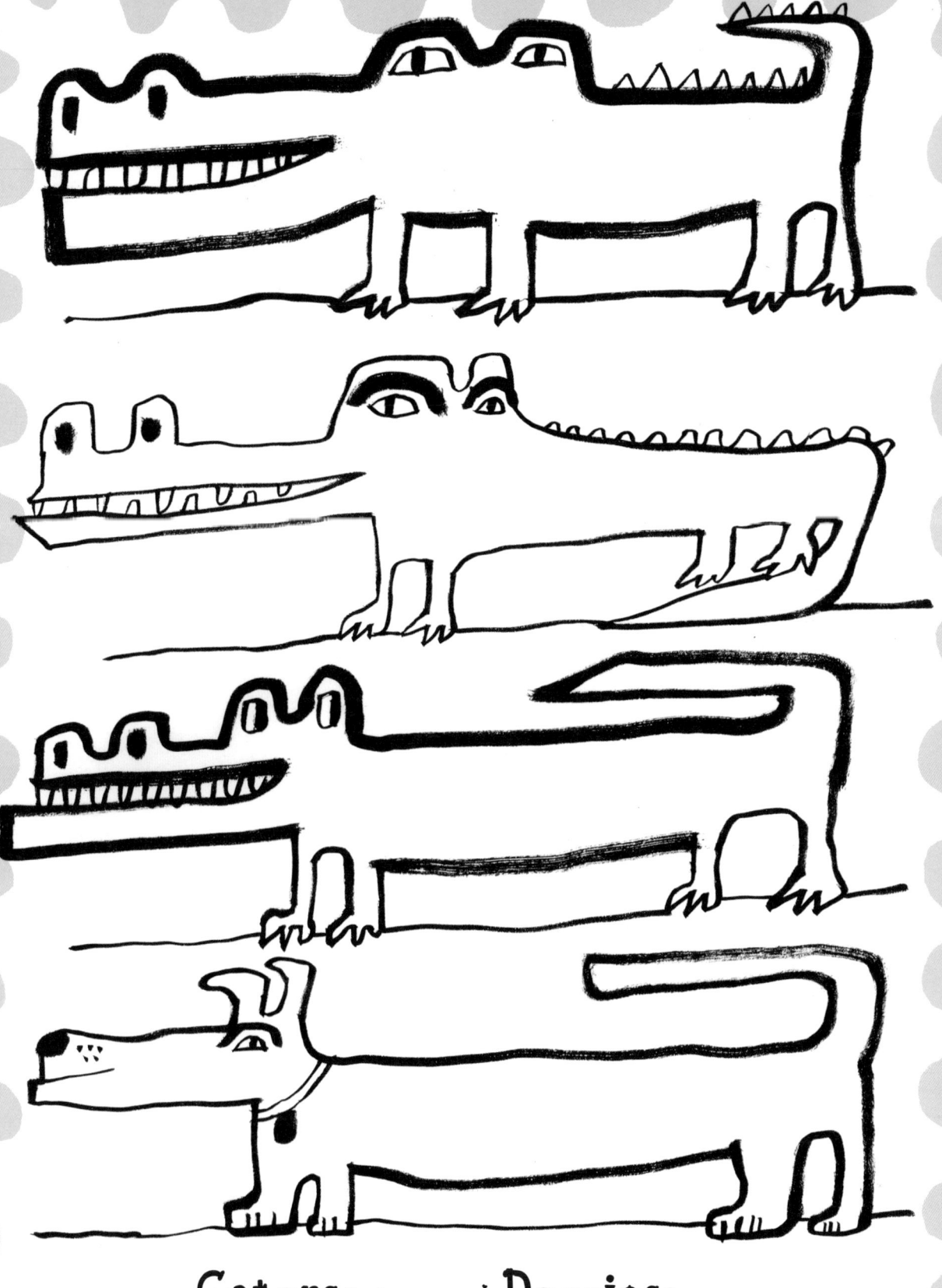

Gators: three and Doggies: one.
Horizontal drawing fun.

Grooving about. No doubt.

Dogs in profile.

Draw one going "woof"
or with an aloof smile.

Fluttergirls and **flutterguys.**
It rhymes with something.
(Big surprise.)

Bird-bugs or
bug-birds?

Drawing two of
each might help you
reach a conclusion.
(Or just cause
confusion.)

Doodle a beetle (on a beetlescooter).

It is, I know, absurd:
a pachedermal beetle-bird.

Giraffe-snail and friend

Beanbodies all!

Sea what?

Slinky slinky slinkycats

Insects made of lines and shapes.
Around the page they hop and traipse.

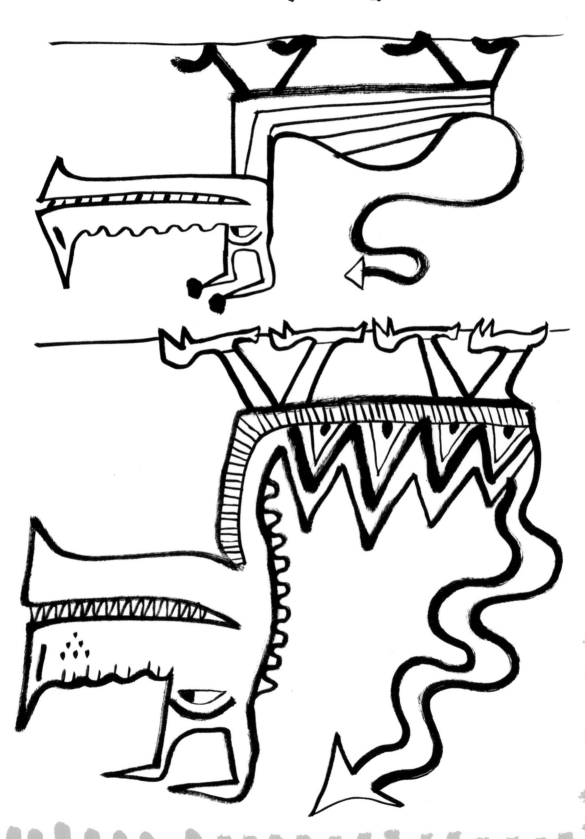

Draw a crazy critter-car!

Zoom it off to Zanzibar!

Here come the **WhirlyturtS!** The helicopterrapins!
Two up there are twins.

Bird is about to
do an awesome trick.
Something sick.

Owls (obviously)

A silly school of swimmy types. Curvy lines and dots and stripes.

You bet!

Can a turtle trio become a quartet,
quintet, sextet, or septet?

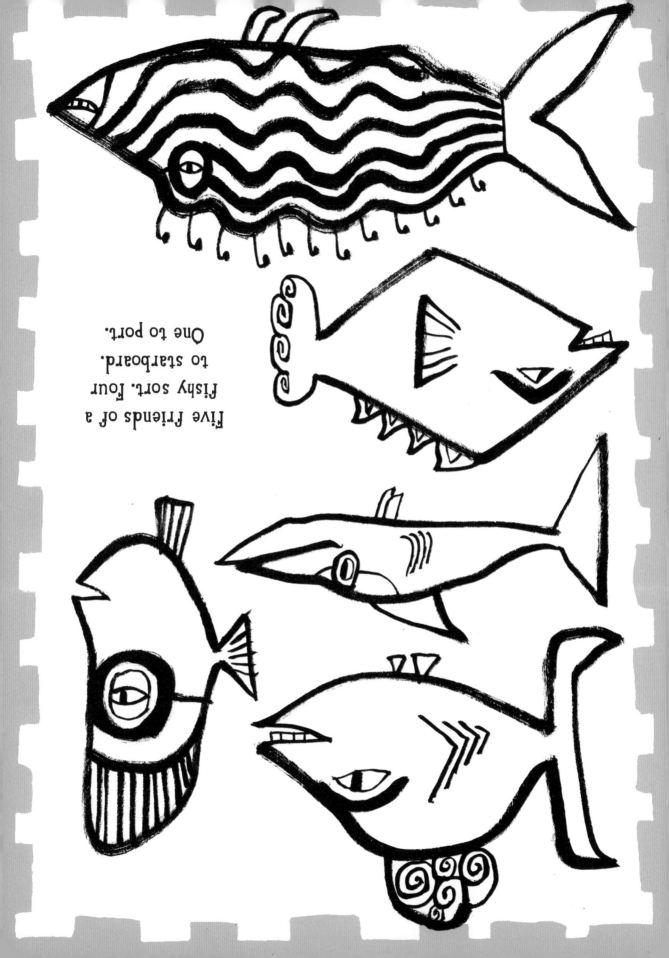

Five friends of a
fishy sort. Four
to starboard.
One to port.

Owlhaus #7609

Silliest creatures
EVER,
according to me.

What are your top three?

Camel, camel, **camelturtle**, camel

Crabs of the
hermit sort

Either paddling or idling—draw a canoer.
The lake needs more, not fewer.

Are you aware of Stairbugs?

Ever gone through phases or crazes of drawing odd vases?

Nothing is sillier than a preposterous proboscis.

Sketch out some bodies to go with the noodles.
Scaly like serpents or fuzzy like poodles.

Many
many moons

Hippo, puppy, gatorbunny. Pick one. Draw it. Make it funny.

A good old-fashioned Gator Race!

Draw some more to set the pace!

Shoecar racers screech and **squeal!**
They stomp on the brakes and they wear down the heel.

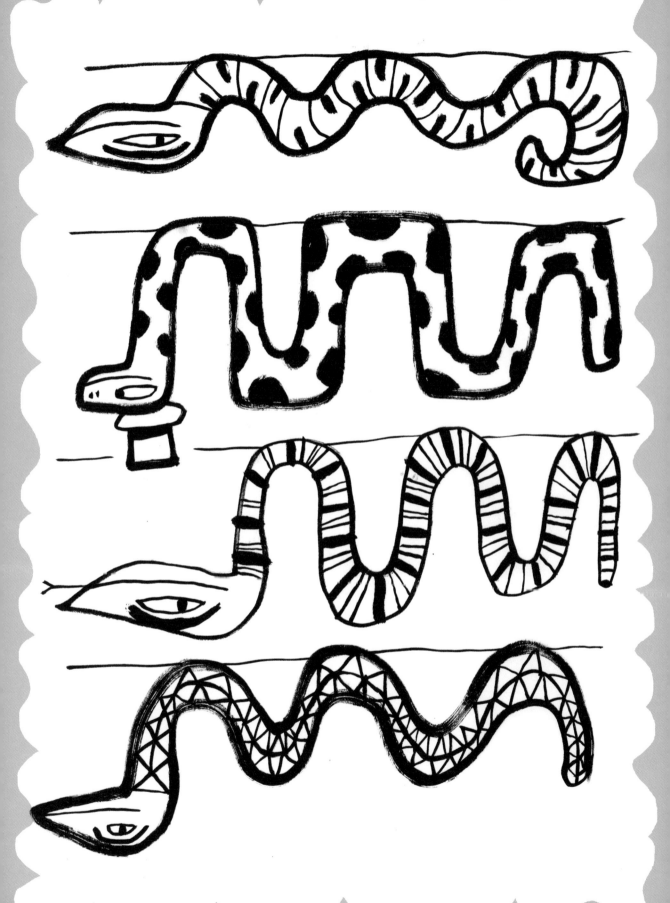

I can hardly wait to create and decorate another locomotive. Are they loco? Sort of.

What will happen,
if, by chance, some others
come to join the dance?

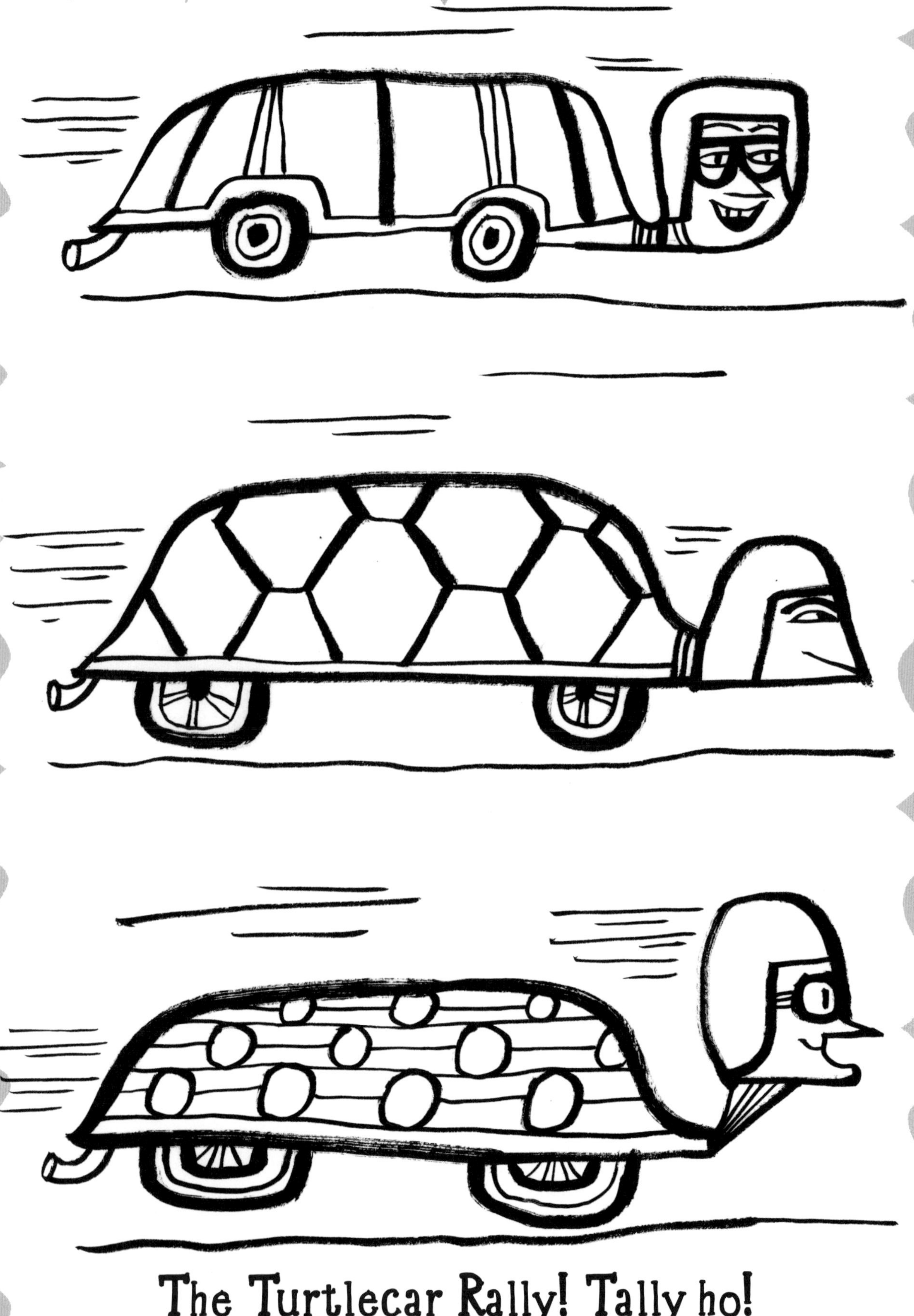

The Turtlecar Rally! Tally ho!

Two went **east** and one went **west**,
In search, perhaps, of hive or nest?

Cat faces facing you.
Draw six, then erase a few.

Totally old-school.

Draw a bug atop a toadstool.

Brickmane Sphinxes

Say hello to the triple-giraffe.

What other creatures make you laugh?

Expressions will vary from Flower to Flower.
Some will smile, and some will glower.

Draw a
friendly
plane.

Give it
a name.

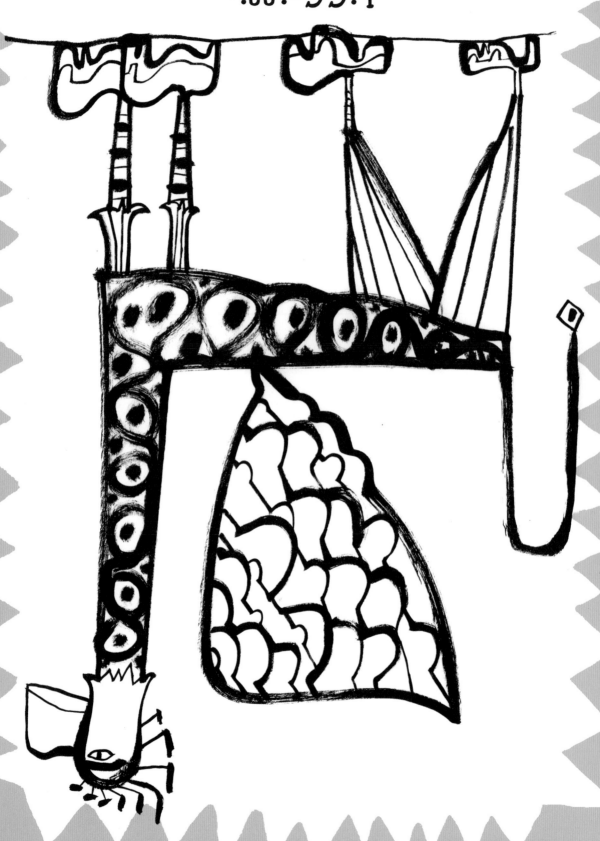

bIGGriffin

Who loves guitars?

Cat Fairy.
Cute?
Very.

Keep drawing, doodling, sketching, and scribbling!
That's an order! No quibbling!

Book design by Kristine Brogno.
Typeset in Calef Bold.
The illustrations in this book were rendered in brush and ink.

Manufactured in China in November 2011.

1 3 5 7 9 10 8 6 4 2

This product conforms to CPSIA 2008.

Chronicle Books LLC
680 Second Street, San Francisco, California 94107

www.chroniclekids.com